To my grandmother 祖母 and aunt 姑姑, looking back;
To Juliette and Tanya, going forward;
And to my mother, always — L.F.

For my beloved homeland, Taiwan — C.W.

Tundra Books, an imprint of Penguin Random House Canada Young Readers, a division of Penguin Random House of Canada Limited.

LIBRARY AND ARCHIVES CANADA CATALOGUING IN PUBLICATION

Title: Ten little dumplings / Larissa Fan ; Cindy Wume, illustrator
Names: Fan, Larissa, author. | Wume, Cindy, illustrator.
Identifiers: Canadiana (print) 20200182358 | Canadiana (ebook) 20200182404 | ISBN 9780735266193 (hardcover) | ISBN 9780735266209 (EPUB)
Subjects: LCGFT: Picture books.
Classification: LCC PS8611.A53 T46 2021 | DDC jC813/.6—dc23

Published simultaneously in the United States of America by Tundra Books of Northern New York, an imprint of Penguin Random House Canada Young Readers, a division of Penguin Random House of Canada Limited.

LIBRARY OF CONGRESS CONTROL NUMBER: 2020933323

Edited by Tara Walker with assistance from Margot Blankier
Designed by John Martz
The artwork in this book was created with ink, gouache and colored pencils.
The text was set in Iowan Old Style.

PRINTED AND BOUND IN CHINA

www.penguinrandomhouse.ca

2 3 4 5   25 24 23 22 21

Penguin
Random House
tundra | TUNDRA BOOKS

TEN LITTLE DUMPLINGS

Words by Larissa Fan · Pictures by Cindy Wume

tundra

In the village of Fengfu,
At the top of the hill,
In a very large house,
There lived a special family.

Special because they had ten sons.
To have one son was considered lucky,
To have ten was great luck indeed!

Their parents called them their ten little dumplings.
Not only because as babies they were round like dumplings,
But also because, like sons, dumplings are auspicious,
Bringing prosperity and success.

The ten brothers did everything together:
Ten getting ready in the morning.

Ten playing by the old fish pond.

Ten eating rice at the big round table.

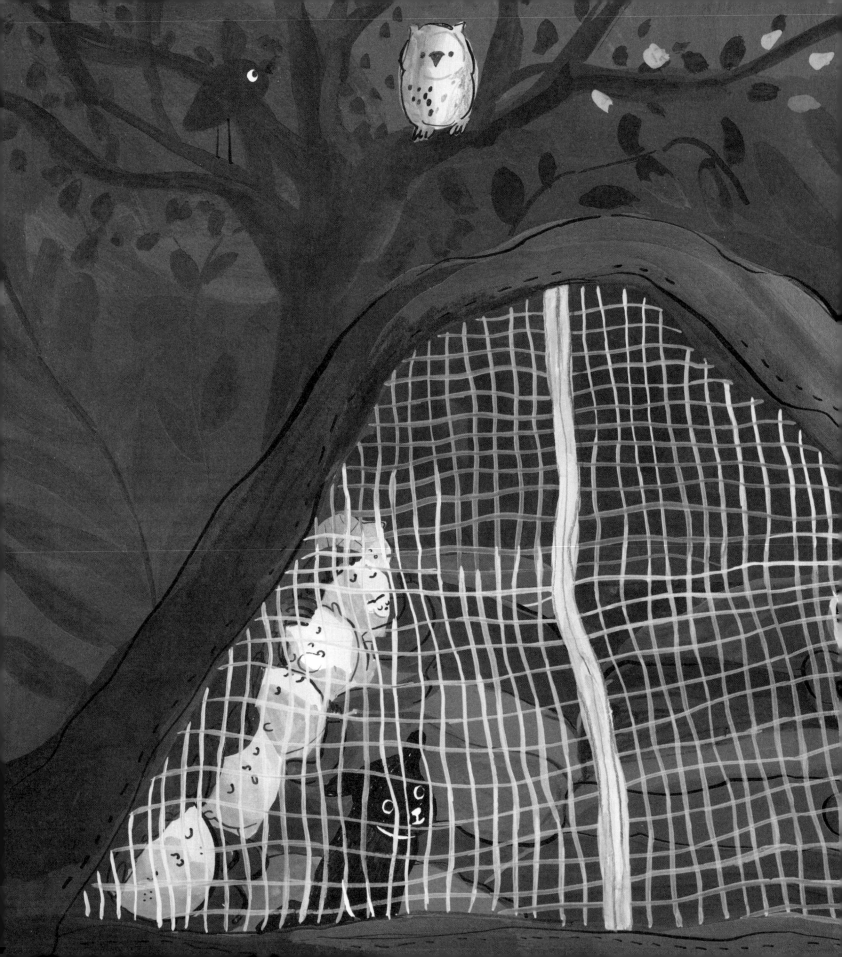

Ten falling asleep by the light of the moon.

Wherever they went, the boys seemed to take luck with them.
The sun shone brighter, the grass grew greener.
They were so well-known that the villagers sang a song about them.

Ten little dumplings
Always top of the class

Ten little dumplings
Running faster
Jumping higher

Ten little dumplings
Their brushstrokes flow like music.

And the ten little dumplings . . .

Grew into ten fine men.
How proud their parents were!
All of their sons successful and respected.

Those dumplings were my brothers.

You may not have seen me,
But I was there too.

You just need to look more closely.

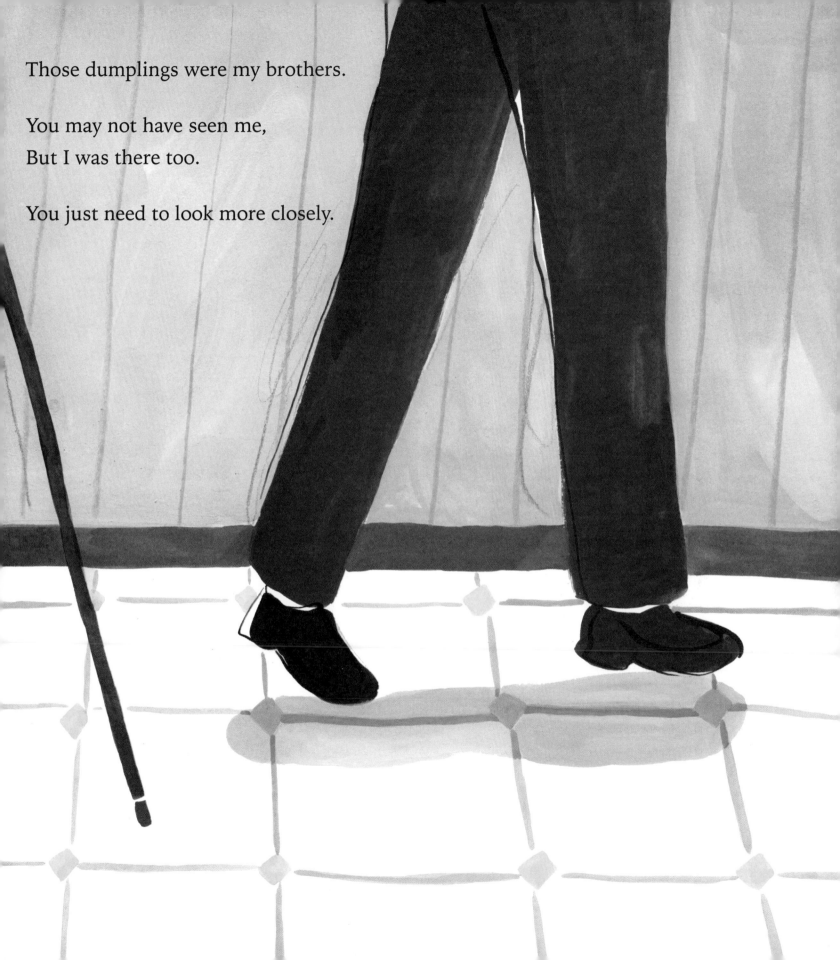

I listened.

I studied.

I learned.

I discovered I had my own talent.

And so I made my way in the world.

Now I'm grown up . . .

And have a child of my own.

My own wonderful girl. My little dumpling.

How lucky I am!

AUTHOR'S NOTE

This story is inspired by my father's family. My father grew up in Taiwan where he was one of ten brothers. Traditionally in Taiwanese culture, sons are prized over daughters. So you can understand why the ten brothers were famous in their small village, and even more so when they all went to university — a truly remarkable feat for a peasant family.

The brothers were compared to an old and well-known Chinese folktale called "Ten Brothers." In this tale, each brother has a special ability, such as great strength or super-keen hearing. Together they battle an adversary and, using their powers, emerge victorious. In modern times, the story has been adapted into cartoons, movies and television shows.

I heard a lot about my father's brothers growing up, and in my mind they took on a kind of mythical status. What I didn't realize until I was older was that my father also had a sister! Learning this made me wonder about who is left out of the stories we are told and why. *Ten Little Dumplings* is my attempt to reveal another viewpoint to a traditional tale, to write in someone who has been left out. I hope you enjoyed her story.